This book is dedicated to our parents and to all parents who take the time to create imaginative stories that their children will never forget.

The weather on the last day of school in Clensiville could not have been more beautiful. The sun was shining brightly, and there was not a cloud to be seen in the clear blue sky.

"We're free!" shouted Tidy as she ran through the school doors for the last time of the year.

"No more spelling tests! No more math problems!" Messy squealed.

The two sisters hurried home with happy thoughts of all the wonderful games they could play and adventures they could find now that summertime had finally come.

When they arrived home, however, they were surprised to find that their little brother, VeryMessy, had made quite a mess out of all their toys. He sat in the mess with a big smile on his face. Their mother welcomed home the two girls with a hug and a kiss.

"I know that it is a beautiful day," said their mother, "but please clean up all of these toys before you go out to play."

"That little monster!" shouted Tidy. "Why do we have to clean up *his* mess?"

"He's just a little kid. He doesn't know any better," explained Messy.

The girls decided that they better do what their mother asked so that they could go outside and play. Each picked a different half of the room to clean in her own special way.

Tidy took her time to make sure everything was lined up perfectly. All the cars were lined up from smallest to largest. All the dolls were neatly dressed and standing upright. The board games were carefully stacked in alphabetical order. Amazing ANTics was all the way on the top and ZigZagZap was on the bottom. Tidy looked at her half of the room and gave a nod of approval. It was **very, very** clean.

Messy's half of the room also looked cleaner than it had before, but not nearly as clean as Tidy's half. There were many piles. All of the balls were together in the same area. The army men had been thrown into a big pile. There was also a gigantic mountain of stuffed animals.

"It's all clean. That means we can go out to play now," said Messy.

"You call *that* clean?" said Tidy. "It is not even close to being as clean as **my** half."

"That's okay, it is clean enough. Not everything has to be perfectly clean," Messy replied. "Anyway, now we can go out and play. But where is VeryMessy?"

There he is!

Now that all the toys had been cleaned up, Tidy, Messy, and VeryMessy went outside to play on their first day of summer vacation.

"Let's go on an adventure into the woods," Messy suggested.

"You *know* we're not supposed to go into the woods!" replied Tidy.

"But our backyard is too small," said Messy. "Besides, we won't stay long and Mom will never find out."

"I don't know about this . . . " started Tidy, but it was too late. Messy was already walking towards the woods, with VeryMessy not far behind.

By the time Tidy caught up to her brother and sister, they were already deep into the woods. The sun had disappeared behind the thick trees that now towered over the children.

The woods seemed to be alive all around them, and they heard strange and eerie sounds of unknown creatures.

After walking for a bit, Tidy stopped. "You don't even know where we are going, do you?" she asked.

"Sure I do," replied Messy. "We are going on an adventure."

"But do you even know which way we *came* from?"

Messy looked around. "Um . . . that way?" she guessed.

Tidy looked **very** unhappy with her sister. "You got us lost!" she said. "You just ran into the woods without even knowing where you were going. *And* you got me and *your* little brother lost too! He just follows you wherever you go and -- " she stopped. "Where is VeryMessy?"

"VeryMessy!" the girls shouted.

"Where are youuuuuu?"

When the girls finally found VeryMessy, he was up to some **very messy** behavior, indeed. He had found a beehive. There was honey all over his fingers and clothes. When he saw the girls, he gave them a big, honey-covered smile.

"*Gross,*" said Tidy. "How are we ever going to get him clean?"

"There is no such thing as a clean VeryMessy," said Messy.

Tidy knew her sister was right.

All of a sudden, a swarm of bees came buzzing back to the beehive. They were not very happy to find that they had visitors. The bees flew all around the children.

"Ruuuun!" shouted Messy. They ran as fast as their legs could take them.

"Ouch!" Tidy hollered. She had been stung!

After the children had finally outrun the last of the bees, Tidy said, "This is just *great*. Now we're even more lost than before, and of course, *I'm* the one who got stung."

"Does it hurt?" asked Messy, concerned for her sister.

"No," said Tidy. She put on her bravest face and pulled out the stinger.

"That looked like it hurt," said Messy.

"I'll be fine," said Tidy. "Let's just get out of here!"

Tidy, Messy, and VeryMessy walked and walked but couldn't seem to find their way back home. They walked by trees, bushes, and rocks, but they all looked the same.

"Didn't we already pass that rock?" Messy asked.

"You're right, I think we're walking in circles," Tidy groaned.

"We never should have gone into the woods," said Messy. "I just wish we were in our safe backyard right now."

VeryMessy tugged on Tidy's skirt and pointed to the trees. "What is it, VeryMessy? What do you see?"

A bear!

"ROARRR," snarled the grizzly bear as it came rumbling through the trees. The three children yelled in fear.

Not knowing what to do, Tidy picked up her baby brother and started running in the opposite direction, with Messy not far behind.

They ran as fast as they could through the woods as the trees whizzed by.

Finally, they could no longer hear the bear behind them.

Out of breath, Messy stopped and said, "I think
. . . we . . . outran . . . " but before she could
finish what she was saying, she was staring at
another bear.

She screamed and turned to run the other way,
but the first bear had caught up.

They were trapped!

Both of the bears stood upright and opened their mouths wide, revealing many sharp teeth. The children were very scared.

"What do we do?" whimpered Messy.

"I have an idea!" exclaimed Tidy.

Quickly, Tidy put her brother down and began taking off his shirt and shorts, leaving him wearing only his diaper.

"But Tidy, I don't think that the bears are going to be afraid of a naked baby," said Messy.

"No they won't," said Tidy, "But they'll just *love* VeryMessy's honey-covered shirt! It's a good thing he messed with those bees after all!"

With that, Tidy tossed the clothes into a little pile and waited to see what the bears would do.

As the three children inched away from the pile of honey-covered clothes, the bears began snorting and sniffing. They came upon the pile of clothes and began licking and slurping them.

The bears enjoyed the sweet taste of honey so much that they completely forgot about the children!

Tidy, Messy, and VeryMessy walked away faster and faster until they were sprinting away from the bears.

The children ran a bit longer, and then finally found their way home to their safe backyard.

"We made it!" exclaimed Tidy.

"Thanks to you and your smart thinking," said Messy. "If you hadn't distracted them with the honey, we might be in their bellies instead of VeryMessy's clothes."

"That's true," said Tidy, "but if VeryMessy wasn't very messy then we wouldn't have been able to turn his clothes into bear snacks. Speaking of VeryMessy, where is he?"

The girls walked inside to find that VeryMessy had already made a complete mess of all the toys that they had cleaned up earlier that day. Tidy's neat rows and stacks had been knocked into piles, and Messy's piles of toys had been scattered throughout the room.

Their mother walked into the room and scolded them. "I thought I told you children to clean up this room! Clean it up, or I won't let you go outside and play!"

The girls looked at each other and laughed. "That's just fine with us," they said as they watched VeryMessy doing what he did best.

Made in the USA
San Bernardino, CA
16 October 2018